Elizabeth Creith   Linda Hendry

Erik the Viking Sheep

Scholastic Canada Ltd.

Toronto, New York, London, Sydney, Auckland

This book is dedicated with love and friendship to Nancy Pease, who introduced me to Viking sheep, and to Bill Richardson, for his unfailing support and encouragement.

– EC

For Anna and Katherine, my little lambs.

– LH

This book was designed in QuarkXPress
with type set in 18-point Stempel Schneidler Medium.

The illustrations were painted in watercolours on Arches paper

Canadian Cataloguing in Publication Data
Creith, Elizabeth
Erik the Viking sheep
ISBN 0-590-12380-7
I. Title.
PS8555.R446E74 1997   jC318i.54   C97-930369-9
PZ7.C73Er 1997

5 4 3 2 1   Printed and Bound in Canada   7 8 9 /9

Once there was a sheep.

He was a lonely sheep, in a pen all by himself. All the other sheep were off in a field together. He could see them, but he couldn't talk to them. He had just arrived at this farm after a long journey, and he wanted company.

At first the only company he had was the woman who came to feed him. One day she brought a little girl with her.

"He looks different from the other sheep, Mom," said the girl. "And he's red."

"He *is* different, Marie," said her mother. "He's an Icelandic sheep, and he's just come from Iceland. This breed is more than a thousand years old. The Vikings used to keep sheep like him."

"Wow!" said Marie, "a Viking sheep! We could call him Erik the Red!"

"If you like," said her mother, smiling.

"But why is he all alone in here?" asked Marie.

"He's in quarantine," said her mother. "That means he has to stay away from the other sheep until we know he isn't sick with something. Sometimes you can't tell right away."

"Poor Erik," said Marie. "I'll come and visit you."

Erik now had a name, but better than that, he had some company. Marie came every day after school and read to him about the Vikings. She brought a book with pictures of big, hairy men wearing flapping cloaks and helmets with horns. They carried swords and shields, and rode across the water on dragon-headed ships. Marie sat on the ground and leaned against the fence to read, and Erik looked over the fence at the pictures.

Marie couldn't be there all the time.
Erik was still alone a lot. But now, when
he was by himself, he imagined himself as
Erik the Viking Sheep. He would wear
a splendid cloak and a fierce helmet
— he already had the horns —
and ride at the front of his great
dragon-headed ship. He would have
a sword and shield. He was a little
confused about what he would do with
them, since hooves aren't very good for
holding things. But a Viking had to have a
sword and shield, so Erik the Viking
Sheep would have them, too.

Erik imagined himself leading a shipload of fierce Viking sheep on a raid. They would steal all the hay and grain, and kidnap young ewes. They would look so fierce in their helmets and cloaks that everybody would be afraid of them. Then they would sail away before anybody could stop them, and bring their booty back to the farm.

Day after day, Erik imagined this story while he waited for Marie to come and read to him.

One day the woman came and let him into the bigger field. Erik was very excited. Now he would have other sheep for company. He could tell them his story about being Erik the Viking Sheep. Maybe they could even form a flock of Vikings and go raiding — with Erik as the leader, of course.

At first the other sheep listened politely when Erik talked, but they weren't very interested. They liked grazing and lying peacefully in the shade. Erik wouldn't let them lie peacefully. He talked about Vikings all the time. The other sheep began to be rude to him.

"Go away!" they said when he started to talk. Sometimes they butted him. Then they started to run away whenever he came near.

The oldest ewe tried to talk some sense into Erik.
"We sheep don't like new ideas," she said,
"and we don't like going to strange places. It upsets us
when you talk like this. It gives us indigestion."
As sheep have more than one stomach, indigestion
is a serious thing for them.

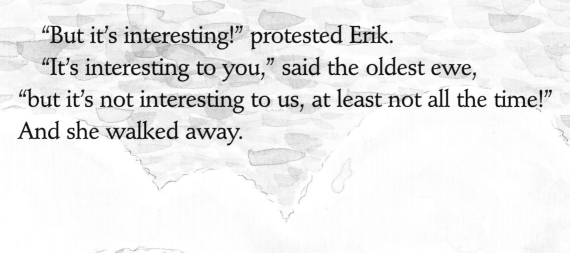

"But it's interesting!" protested Erik.
"It's interesting to you," said the oldest ewe,
"but it's not interesting to us, at least not all the time!"
And she walked away.

But Erik couldn't seem to help himself. He kept thinking about Viking sheep, and he kept talking about Viking sheep. And soon he had lots of time to think about them because none of the others would come near him.

One day Eric found a bucket, and he got an idea. "If I put my head right in the bucket," he thought, "I could find out what it's like to wear a helmet. I could find out what it's really like to be Erik the Viking Sheep!"

So he put his head in the bucket, right down to the bottom. It was dark, and his breathing echoed in the bucket, and he didn't think he liked it much. But when he tried to pull his head out . . . the bucket was stuck! The handle had flipped down over one of his horns, and he couldn't unstick it!

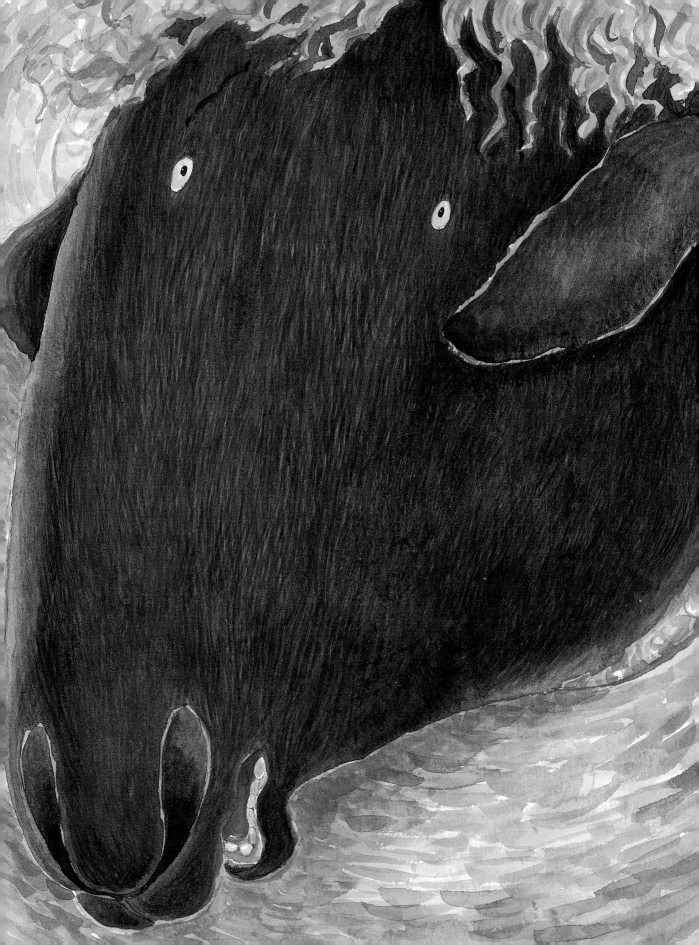

Erik panicked. He couldn't see where he was going. He blundered around, crashing into the fence and tripping over uneven ground.

Then suddenly — SPLASH!
The bucket fell off his head. He was standing in
the pond, in water almost up to his neck. The ducks
on the pond swam around, laughing at him.

"*Wack, wack, wack!*" laughed the ducks. "*Wack, wack!
Sheep don't swim!*"

The other sheep had come running when they saw Erik with the bucket on his head. Sheep are very curious. So when Erik turned around to climb out of the pond, he saw them all standing there, laughing.

"Erik the Viking Shee-eep! Erik the Viking Shee-eep!" some of them sang.

"Hey, Erik the Viking Sheep, where's your dragon ship?" one shouted. And they all laughed and laughed.

Erik struggled out of the pond and walked away to the farthest corner of the field. He stood there a long time, feeling very bedraggled and embarrassed — and lonely.

After a while the oldest ewe came up beside him. She pretended to graze for a few minutes and then she said, "Come on, we're all going over to the salt lick."

"I can't," said Erik, "they'll laugh."

"No, they won't," said the oldest ewe. "We've laughed at you once, and I think you've learned your lesson. Most sheep don't like to think about new things — it gives us indigestion. But we don't mind a little excitement, once in a while. Just don't talk our ears off about Viking sheep anymore."

"All right," agreed Erik. And he kept his word. It wasn't very hard, because he knew if he even said the words "Viking sheep" everyone would remember him in the duck pond and start giggling. Erik found that it was quite nice to have the company of other sheep, and to lie peacefully in the shade.

After a few days, one of the lambs came over and asked him shyly, "Um, Erik, would you tell us the part about the ship again?"

"Oh," said another lamb, "and the part about, you know, the helmets? We'd like to hear that again."

"Really?" asked Eric.

"Yes, really!" said the lambs.

So Erik began to tell his Viking sheep story, and by the time he finished, all the lambs were listening, and some of the grown-up sheep, too.

He began to think of other stories, and to tell
them to the lambs sometimes in the afternoons.
He became the best storyteller in the flock,
and told many different stories, although
the one about Erik the Viking Sheep
was secretly his favourite.

But he was always very careful
about buckets.